Seymour Simon

SEE
MORE
READERS

AMAZING AIRCRAFT

SeaStar Books • New York

This book is dedicated to Joel and Benjamin.

Cover photograph: Two super-light personal aircraft, the Defiant (top) and the Boomerang (bottom), by experimental designer Burt Rutan

Title page photograph: A Fokker triplane (top) and a Sopwith Pup biplane (bottom) at a recent air show

Opposite page photograph: A hang glider

Special thanks to reading consultant Dr. Linda B. Gambrell, Director, School of Education, Clemson University. Dr. Gambrell has served as President of the National Reading Conference and Board Member of the International Reading Association.

Permission to use the following photographs is gratefully acknowledged: front cover: © James A. Sugar/CORBIS; title page: © Dick Hanley, Photo Reseachers, Inc.; pages 2–3: © Peter Poby/CORBIS; pages 4–5: © Erich Nebel; pages 6–9, 12–13: © Bettmann/CORBIS; pages 10–11: © CORBIS; pages 14–15: © Underwood & Underwood/CORBIS; pages 16–19: © Hulton–Deutsch/CORBIS; pages 20–21: © Dewitt Jones/CORBIS; pages 22–23: © The Military Picture Library/CORBIS; pages 24–25: © Kit Kittle/CORBIS; pages 26–27: © De Malglaive/Explorer, Photo Researchers, Inc.; pages 28–29: © Aero Graphics, Inc./CORBIS; pages 30–31: © AFP/CORBIS; page 32: © Charles O'Rear/CORBIS.

Library of Congress Cataloging-in-Publication Data is available.
ISBN 1-58717-179-1 (reinforced trade edition)
1 3 5 7 9 RTE 10 8 6 4 2
ISBN 1-58717-180-5 (paperback edition)
1 3 5 7 9 PB 10 8 6 4 2
PRINTED IN SINGAPORE BY TIEN WAH PRESS
For more information about our books, and the authors and artists who create them, visit our web site: www.northsouth.com

People have always wanted to fly.

The great scientist
Leonardo da Vinci drew plans
for flapping wing machines
in 1487, over 500 years ago.
But the first flight took place
in France in 1783.
The pilot was carried into the air
in a hot-air balloon that drifted
with the wind.

Two brothers, Wilbur and Orville
Wright, made the first flights
powered by an engine.
On December 17, 1903,
their plane took off
from the sand dunes
at Kitty Hawk, North Carolina.

The longest flight lasted less than a minute and went 852 feet at a speed of 30 miles per hour.

Early airplanes had thin wings covered with cloth. In 1909, Louis Blériot took off from France and flew 20 miles across the English Channel.

His flight took 36 minutes.
Today you can fly the same
distance in less than 3 minutes.

American pilot Charles Lindbergh was the first to fly alone, nonstop, across the Atlantic Ocean. His plane, *The Spirit of St. Louis*, took off from Long Island on May 20, 1927.

Nearly 34 hours later, he landed in Paris after flying 3,610 miles. Today, airliners fly from New York to Paris in less than 7 hours.

The *Hindenburg*
was an 800-foot-long airship
filled with hydrogen gas.
That is more than three times
as long as today's 747 airplanes.
The Hindenburg carried
nearly 100 passengers
across the Atlantic Ocean.
But in 1937 it burst into flames
while landing in New Jersey.
Many people died in the explosion.

Planes that take off from and land on water are called seaplanes. The most famous flying boats were the Pan American Clippers in the late 1930s.

The Clippers had four engines and
flew almost 200 miles per hour.

The Spitfire was a British fighter
plane during World War II.
It carried two cannons and
four machine guns in its wings.
Spitfires were used to attack
German bomber planes.
In 1940, Britain's Royal Air Force
shot down so many German planes
that the invasion of England
was cancelled.

The Douglas DC-3 was the first
inexpensive passenger plane.
DC-3s carried twenty passengers
at 200 miles per hour for distances
of up to 1,500 miles.
During World War II, DC-3s were
used to carry parachute troops.
After the war, thousands of DC-3s
were used to carry passengers
all over the world.

The Boeing 747
made its first flight in 1969.
It carried nearly 500 passengers at
speeds of over 500 miles per hour.
The 747 can stay in the air
for 17 hours and travel
more than 8,000 miles.
The plane itself is longer
than the distance of
the Wright Brothers' first flight.

Helicopters have spinning wings
on top called rotors.
They can take off straight up into
the air and land straight down.

Helicopters are used for medical
emergencies and police work.
They also carry military troops
and construction machines.
The biggest helicopters can lift
over 80,000 pounds on one flight.

Gliders are lightweight planes
that have no motors.
Instead, they float on air currents.
Small hang gliders can be
launched from the tops of hills
and mountains.
Big gliders are towed up into
the air by planes with engines
and then set free.

The Concorde supersonic jet flies at over 1,300 miles per hour, more than twice the speed of sound. A Concorde can fly from New York to London in three hours, less than half the time of a 747.

The Lockheed F-117 is a "stealth" fighter plane. Stealth means that the F-117 is hard to see on radar. That's because its black, flat surfaces absorb radar waves instead of bouncing them back. At night, the F-117 is almost invisible in every way.

In the future there will be
huge planes that can carry
up to 800 passengers,
nearly twice as many as a 747.

The wings on this new cargo plane
are over 250 feet long,
almost the length of a football field.

It once took people weeks or months to travel to distant places by boat, train, car, or bus. Today we can fly to these places in a day or even a few hours. Aircraft have shrunk the world.